# Ladybug Girl

and

## Bumblebee Boy

by David Soman and Jacky Davis

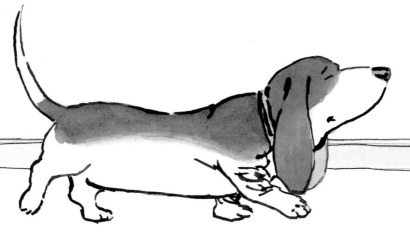

SCHOLASTIC INC.

New York  Toronto  London  Auckland

Sydney  Mexico City  New Delhi  Hong Kong

For Benjamin and Netanya, Super-Heroes

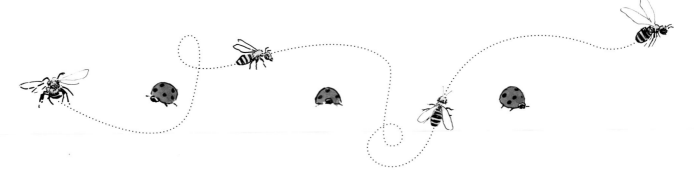

ISBN 978-0-545-25508-0

12 11 10 9 8 7 6 5 4 3 2 1          10 11 12 13 14 15/0

Printed in Singapore          46

First Scholastic printing, April 2010

Designed by Teresa Dikun and Jasmin Rubero
Text set in Aunt Mildred

"Ladybug Girl is ready to play!"
says Lulu.
She has been waiting **forever** to go to
her favorite playground—the one with the
**twisty slide** and
        the **bouncy dinosaurs.**

Her mama grabs Bingo's leash and says,
"All right, let's go!"

Ladybug Girl leaps over sidewalk cracks
that are as big as canyons.
When she sees Mrs. Robbins carrying her groceries,
Ladybug Girl swoops over to help.
The bag is as heavy as a boulder,
but it isn't a problem for
Ladybug Girl.

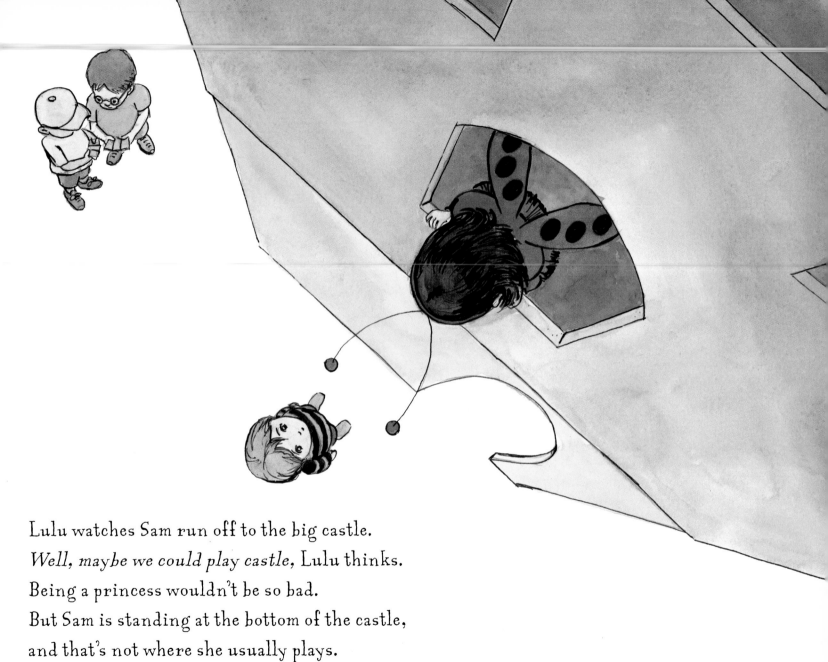

Lulu watches Sam run off to the big castle.
*Well, maybe we could play castle,* Lulu thinks.
Being a princess wouldn't be so bad.
But Sam is standing at the bottom of the castle,
and that's not where she usually plays.
"Why are you down **there**?" Lulu asks, puzzled.
"Don't you think playing on the **top** is better?"

When Sam doesn't answer, Lulu says,
"Never mind, I know the perfect thing for us to do!
The seesaw!" She runs over and
sits down on one side of the seesaw

and waits.

And waits.

Sam just stands there, not getting on.
The other side is high and empty
while she is stuck on the ground.

"I'll show you!" she says.
"Ladybug Girl has superpowers!
I can fly and I'm superstrong!"

"Superpowers?"
Sam is very interested.

"And who can I be?" he asks.

"Well, you sort of look like a bee . . ." says Lulu.

"A bee? Yeah! A bee can fly!

And he will sting people if they bother him!

I need a stinger . . ." says Sam.

He sees a stick and picks it up.

"I'm Bumblebee Boy!"
Sam declares.
"And I'm Ladybug Girl!"
yells Lulu.

"Nothing can stop us!"

Ladybug Girl and Bumblebee Boy zoom around the playground looking to help anyone in trouble. A squirrel scampers by Bingo.

"Oh no!" yells Bumblebee Boy.
"That Scary Monster is trying to get your dog! He needs our help right away!"

"We're coming, Bingo!"
says Bumblebee Boy.
They bravely charge forward.
The Scary Monster is no match for their
superpowers and leaps away.

"We did it!
We saved Bingo!
Are you okay?" asks
Ladybug Girl.
Bingo wags his tail.

Then Bumblebee Boy runs toward the swings.

"Watch how high I can fly!" he yells.

"I can fly high too!" Ladybug Girl says, running behind him.

They are soon whipping through the air.

They flap their wings harder and harder.

They are so high, they can almost touch a cloud.

"Look!" says Ladybug Girl, waving toward the tire swing. "There's a Mean Robot! It's going to crush the playground! We need to stop it!"

They rush over to the Mean Robot. Ladybug Girl grabs on, and jumps on top of its head! Bumblebee Boy stings it with his stinger again and again.

"This will teach you not to mess with Bumblebee Boy!"

"If we're going to play together," says Ladybug Girl, "we don't fight **each other.**"
"Yeah, we work together to fight **bad guys,**
like that Giant Snake over there!"
says Bumblebee Boy, pointing at the twisty slide.
Ladybug Girl adds,
"And Dragonfly Girl can breathe fire!"
"Fire?! I'm Dragonfly Girl!" agrees Marley.

As **Dragonfly Girl** breathes fire,
Ladybug Girl yells,

"Watch out, you big Giant Snake! Here comes the Bug Squad!"

Later, when it's time to go, Lulu says, "It was fun playing together."

"Do you want to play Bug Squad tomorrow?" asks Sam.

"Definitely! Because Ladybug Girl and Bumblebee Boy can do anything!"

"Mama," asks Lulu as they head home, "can we get wings for Bingo?"